Morris Has a Birthday Party!

Written and Illustrated by BERNARD WISEMAN

Little, Brown and Company

BOSTON   TORONTO

To Christina

TEXT AND ILLUSTRATIONS COPYRIGHT © 1983 BY BERNARD WISEMAN

FIRST EDITION

Library of Congress Cataloging in Publication Data

Wiseman, Bernard.
  Morris has a birthday party!

  Summary: Despite many misunderstandings, Boris the Bear and two children give a birthday party for Morris the Moose.
  [1. Birthdays — Fiction.   2. Parties — Fiction.
3. Animals — Fiction]   I. Title.
PZ7.W7802Mon   1983   [E]   82-22860
ISBN 0-316-94854-3

*Published simultaneously in Canada
by Little, Brown & Company (Canada) Limited*

PRINTED IN THE UNITED STATES OF AMERICA

Boris the Bear said,
"I saw a BIG birthday cake!"

Morris the Moose asked,
"Did it SCARE you?"

"No," said Boris. "Birthday cakes cannot scare you."

Morris asked, "Don't they bite?"

"No," said Boris. "Let me tell you
about birthday cakes—
they are good to eat . . .
they say HAPPY BIRTHDAY . . ."

Morris asked, "What do they say
when you eat them?"

Boris cried,
"Birthday cakes cannot talk!"

"Then how can they say
HAPPY BIRTHDAY?" asked Morris.

Boris shouted,
"They say it in writing!"

Morris said,
"Birthday cakes cannot talk.
How did they learn to write?"

Boris roared,
"Birthday cakes cannot write!
They—Ohhh! Come with me—
I will SHOW you
what birthday cakes are."

"Look—" said Boris. "There is
the big birthday cake.
There are other birthday cakes.
Do you see what they are?"

"Yes!" Morris yelled. "And I see
they look good to eat!
I WANT A BIRTHDAY CAKE!"

A boy named Tom said,
"That moose wants
a birthday cake.
It must be his BIRTHDAY!"

Tom's friend Laura said,
"Let's ask our parents for money.
Let's get him a cake.
Let's have a birthday party!"

Laura yelled, "Moose!
We are going to have
a birthday party! Wait here—
we will call you and the bear
when we are ready."

Soon the children
called Morris and Boris.
Laura said, "Here—
put on funny hats."

Morris said,
"Boris should wear TWO hats.
He might eat too much
of the birthday cake!"

Boris growled,
"You need MORE than two hats!"

Laura cried, "Let's give the presents!"

Tom said, "Here is a pogo stick.
You hop on it—like this.
Happy birthday!"

Morris said,
"You mean, 'HOPPY birthday.' "

A girl named Sally said,
"Here is a Hula-Hoop.
Happy birthday!"

Morris said,
"You mean, 'HOOPY birthday.' "

A girl named Judy said,
"Here is a teddy bear.
Happy birthday!"

Morris said,
"You mean, 'Happy BEARthday.' "

Morris got a bike.

"Oh!" Morris yelled.

"This looks like me!"

Morris got a football.

Boris said, "Look—now the bike
looks MORE like you."

Morris squeezed the horn
on the bike. "Listen—" said Morris.
"It SOUNDS like YOU!"

Laura cried, "I think it is time for
some magic—Tom, do some magic!"

Tom said, "I will make this apple disappear. Presto . . . Magico!"

The apple disappeared.

Morris said, "I can do THAT.
Presto . . . Magico!"

Morris made an apple disappear.

Morris asked,
"Do you want me to make the
birthday cake disappear?"

The children yelled, "No! No!"
Boris growled, "NO!"

Laura cried, "Let's play
Pin-the-Tail-on-the-Donkey!"

Morris said, "I know
a better place to pin it—"

"—Boris needs a longer tail."

Laura cried, "I think it is time
for the birthday cake!"
She asked Morris,
"How old are you?
We must put one candle
on the cake for each year."

"For each what?" asked Morris.

Laura said, "Each YEAR.
Don't you know what years are?"

"Yes," said Morris.
"They are what we HEAR with."

Boris said,
"I will find out how old he is."

Boris asked Morris,
"How many summers
do you remember?"

Morris said, "ALL of them."

Boris cried,
"How many is all of them?
Count the summers!"

Morris counted, "1, 2, 3, 4, 5, 6."
He said,
"I remember SIX summers."

Laura said,
"Then you are six years old.
I will put seven candles
on your birthday cake.
One is for good luck."

Boris said,
"Now I will light the candles."

"Why?" asked Morris.
"It is not DARK yet."

Boris shouted,
"I must light the candles!
You must make a wish!
Then you must
blow out all the candles!"

"Why?" asked Morris.
"You just LIT them."

Boris roared, "MAKE A WISH!"

Morris made a wish.

Boris roared,
"BLOW OUT ALL THE CANDLES!"

Morris blew out all the candles.

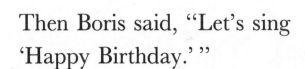

Then Boris said, "Let's sing
'Happy Birthday.' "

Morris asked, "May I sing too?"

"Yes," said Boris. "You may sing.
But you must sing,
'Happy birthday to ME.' "

Morris asked, "Why should I sing
'Happy Birthday' to YOU?
It is not YOUR birthday."

Boris cried, "I don't want you
to sing 'Happy Birthday' to ME!
I want you to sing
'Happy Birthday' to YOU.
So you have to sing,
'Happy birthday to ME!' "

Morris sang,
"Happy birthday to US—
Happy birthday to US!"

Tom yelled, "Now let's eat
the birthday cake!"

"Yes," said Boris. "Then we must
do something we forgot—"

Morris asked,
"What did you forget?"

Boris laughed.
"We forgot to SPANK you!
When you have
a birthday party,
you MUST get SPANKED!"

Morris yelled, "Thank you for
the birthday party and presents!
I will eat my cake on the way home.
I hope my wish comes true. I wished
I could have a birthday EVERY DAY!
Birthdays are FUN!"